AUTHOR'S NOTE

At Christmastime, in the New Hampshire town where I live, it is traditional for white electric candles to be put in house windows and in the windows of the Baptist Church. It is a beautiful sight. But the early residents of this New England town and other villages weren't always so festive. Although Catholics, Episcopalians, Lutherans and some other settlers celebrated Christmas in church and out, the early Baptists, Presbyterians, Quakers, and Puritans tended to avoid any observance of the holiday whatsoever. In fact, one source tells of an Irishman being chased out of a New England town in 1755 because he was "a Christmas Man." All of this set me to thinking, "What *might* have happened in the early 1800s if a family accustomed to celebrating Christmas moved into a New England town?"

Using historical fact and my research as a departure point, I began to imagine that it could have happened this way . . .

T.deP.
NEW HAMPSHIRE

AN
Early American
Christmas

written and illustrated by

Tomie dePaola

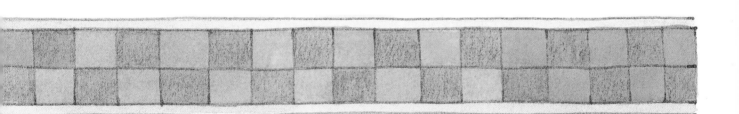

Holiday House : New York

To all the Christmas families
in New London, New Hampshire

Library of Congress Cataloging-in-Publication Data

DePaola, Tomie.
An early American Christmas.

Summary: The inhabitants of a New England village
never make much fuss about Christmas until a new family
moves in and celebrates the holiday in a special way.
[1. Christmas—Fiction]   I. Title.
PZ7.D439Ear   1987   [E]   86-3102
ISBN 0-8234-0617-2
ISBN 0-8234-0979-1 (pbk.)

Once, a long time ago
in the small New England village,
not one single candle could be seen in the windows
at Christmastime.

Not an evergreen wreath on the door.

Not a Christmas tree in the parlor.

Not even a Christmas song could be heard
in the night air . . .

Until the family moved into the white farmhouse
down the road.
They had come first from faraway Germany
to faraway Pennsylvania and finally to this village.

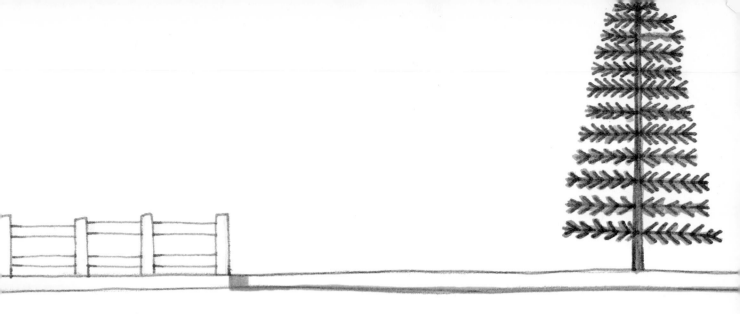

They celebrated Christmas,
so people called them "the Christmas Family."

In the fall of the year,
the young woman and the girl picked
the gray waxy berries
from the bayberry bushes in the field.
They picked and picked.

Then, they put the berries and some water
in the big black cauldron
that was set over a fire
in the kitchen dooryard.

While the old woman stirred and stirred,
the gray green wax formed,
and the young woman poured it into another kettle.

The two women tied strings on sticks
and dipped them into the wax.
They dipped and dipped and dipped some more
and soon the strings became candles—
candles made from bayberries that smelled oh-so-sweet
and that would burn at the windows
and on the mantelpiece at Christmastime.

"Bayberry candles bring good fortune
to any home where they shed their light,"
said the young woman.

"A bayberry candle burned to the socket
brings luck to the house, food to the larder,
and gold to the pocket," said the old woman.

In the fall of the year,
the young man and the boys gathered the apples
and the pumpkins and the squash,
and they dug the potatoes and put them away for the winter
in the root cellar.
The best apples, the reddest and the shiniest,
were set aside to be used at Christmastime.

The old man carved and whittled
while the baby watched—
a new figure for the manger scene.

As the days grew shorter, the winds blew colder.
Then the snow began to fly and December was here.
Soon, soon, it would be Christmas.

Around the fire the family sat
while scissors snipped out birds and ladies and gentlemen,
and riders on white horses, angels, pomegranates,
"hearts of man" and long bands—
all to trim the Christmas tree.
The girl folded paper into stars
to put on the bushes outside.
She waxed them to protect them from the snow.

The old man turned nuts into golden fruit
with a flick of his brush,
and the old woman baked the cookies
that would hang beside the golden nuts
on the tree.

Out in the meadow, by the edge of the woods,
the young man and the boys looked for a tree
to cut and bring inside when the time came.
They tied a red cloth to the top
so they would find it again.

Up from the root cellar came apples
to cut and to string and to dry
for garlands to put on the tree.
Corn was popped and set aside for a day,
and then it too was strung.

Then the baking for eating began
because Christmas was getting closer—
white cookies, brown cookies,
cookie ladies and cookie men,
cookies made with anise seed, honey cakes,
small pretzels and large pretzels—
pretzels everywhere.
Now, tulips, lovebirds, "hands-and-hearts,"
peacocks, and stars
filled the shelves and tables of the kitchen.

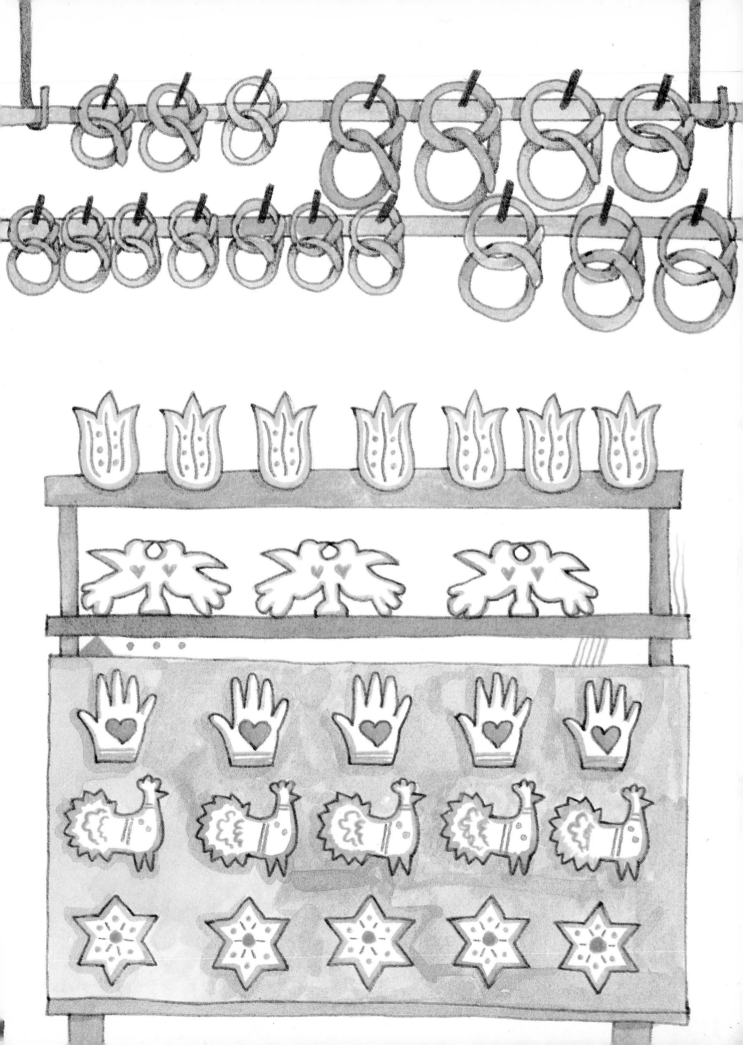

"It's time, it's time,"
   the young man called on the day before Christmas,
   and he and the boys went out to cut the tree
   and gather greens for the mantelpiece
   and the door and the windowsills.

The old man put together the wooden pieces
   for the Christmas pyramid.

The old woman got out the figures
   for the manger scene.

The young woman went to the root cellar
   for the best apples,
   and the girl gathered the candles
   they had made so many days ago.

The baby banged her cup up and down,
   for Christmas was almost here.

In came the tree, into the parlor.

"Quickly, quickly," the old woman said,
"put the greens around, decorate the tree,
   set the manger scene up.
   Candles on the mantelpiece, candles in each window,
   greens on the door,
   waxed paper stars on the bushes outside,
   apples in a rosy pile,
   cookies on platters and plates."

"It's time, it's time," the young woman called.
"It's Christmas Eve, it's time."

Into the parlor the family went.
Then the old man read,
"And it came to pass in those days
    that there went out a decree from Caesar Augustus
    that all the world should be taxed . . ."

The candles were lit,
on the tree and on the mantelpiece.

The candles were lit on the windowsills
to light the way of the Christ Child.

And the neighbors came quietly to look,
and to hear the Christmas songs
coming from the house of "the Christmas Family."

As the years went by,
some of the neighbors put candles in their windows too.
Then Christmas trees appeared in their parlors.
They began to sing Christmas songs.
One by one
every household in the village
became a Christmas family.

"O come let us adore Him. O come let us adore Him . . ."

Urban & Rural Communities
Table of Contents

Urban & Rural Communities: Teacher Tips

What I Think I Know / What I Would Like to Know Activity

A great way to engage children in a new theme is to ask them what they think they know about a subject and what they would like to know about a subject. This activity can be completed as a whole group brainstorming session, in cooperative small groups or independently. Once children have had a chance to contemplate the theme, all information is combined to create a class chart that can be hung up in the classroom. Throughout the study update the chart.

Morning Messages

Morning Messages are intended to provide students with interesting facts about the theme they are studying while also arranging teachable moments in the use of punctuation. Morning Messages are an excellent way to get the "learning going" when the students enter in the morning. The Morning Messages are written in a letter format. There are several ways to present a Morning Message to your class:

Whole Group: Rewrite the morning message on a large sheet of chart paper and allow students to look for the "mistakes" in the letter. The mistakes may be grammar or spelling related. Then as a whole group read the letter together and use it as a springboard for a class discussion.

Individually: As children enter the classroom, give them a copy of the Morning Message and have them fix the "mistakes". The children practice reading the message with a friend until the class is ready to correct the morning message as a group. Use the Morning Message as a springboard for discussion.

Word List

Word lists create a theme related vocabulary. Word lists should be placed on chart paper for students' reference during writing activities. Encourage students to add theme related words. In addition, classify the word list into the categories of nouns, verbs and adjectives.

Urban & Rural Communities: Assessment

Unit Test

At the completion of this unit, students will participate in a paper/pencil unit test to assess their knowledge of the concepts covered. The unit test includes multiple choice and some written answers.

Home Study

Children will collect various items pertaining to their community to add to the class community scrapbook. The purpose of this home study is to acquaint children with their community. The teacher may also wish to send the community scavenger hunt home to be completed.

Constructed Response Learning Logs

Learning logs are an excellent means for students to organize their thoughts and ideas about the urban and rural communities concepts presented. Do not emphasize grammar, spelling or syntax. The student responses give the teacher opportunities to plan activities that may review and clarify concepts learned.

Complete learning log entries on a daily basis or intermittently depending on scheduling. Entries should be brief. Time allotted for completion should be less than fifteen minutes.

Learning logs can include the following kinds of entries:
- Direct instructions by the teacher;
- Key ideas;
- Personal reflections;
- Questions that arise;
- Connections discovered;
- Labeled diagrams and pictures;
- Responses to newspaper articles or television programs, videos etc.

Learning logs can take the form of:
- "What's Your Opinion?" journal prompts;
- Entries In Class Journal;
- Reflective Page.

Student Self-Assessment Rubric:

Students use the rubric to evaluate themselves and the work they produce.

Research Reporting Opportunities

Research reporting opportunities are an excellent way to ensure children have experience in reading informational text and recalling what they have learned in their own words. It is easy to set up a theme related centre by preparing a special table with subject related materials including, books, tapes and magazines etc.

When introducing the children to the use of non-fiction books as a source for their research writing, discuss the different parts usually found in a non- fiction book:

The Title Page: Here you will find the book title and the author's name.

The Table of Contents: Here you will find the name of each chapter, what page it starts on and where you can find specific information.

The Glossary: Here you will find the meaning of special words used in the book.

The Index: Here you will find the ABC list of specific topics you can find in the book.

Next, discuss with the children the criteria of a good research project. It should include:

1. Interesting facts (teacher assigns the number);
2. The use of proper grammar and punctuation, for example, capitals and periods;
3. The size of print so that it is easy to read from faraway;
4. The use of good details in colouring and the drawing of pictures.

Urban & Rural Communities: Expectations

The following expectations are covered in this teacher resource guide.

- Demonstrate an understanding of the of rural and urban communities;

- Use appropriate vocabulary to describe their inquiries and observations;

- Identify the Canadian provinces, territories, and their capitals on a map;

- Make and use large maps of rural and urban communities;

- Consult map legends when looking for selected features;

- Recognize that different colours on maps indicate different things;

- Compare the characteristics of their community to those of a different community;

- Describe the ways in which people interact with other communities;

- Describe ways that communities and people interact with their environment;

- Demonstrate an understanding of why people live where they do (e.g., because of family ties, occupations, amenities, schools);

- Communicate information using oral presentations, written notes and descriptions, tables, charts, and graphs;

- Locate key information about urban and rural communities from primary and secondary sources.

Parent Letter: Urban & Rural Communities

Dear Parents and Guardians,

For the next while, your child will be studying the social studies unit urban and rural communities. The focus of our study will be on identifying distinguishing features of urban and rural communities and describing some possible relationships between these communities.

We will also be creating a class community scrapbook. Look for the information package coming soon.

Families are welcome to contribute to our study by lending any resources such as books, magazines, community artifacts, collections etc,.

Your enthusiastic participation of our class study is greatly appreciated!

Kind regards,

_____

Morning Messages: Urban & Rural Communities

Dear Community Experts,

Did you, know, Some, urban commUnities can have many neighbourhoods? Toronto, Ontario has neighbourhoods known as Chinatown, Greektown, and Little Italy? each of these areas of the city, are unique. Montreal, Quebec and Vancouver, British Columbia are also known for having unique neighbourboods.

Think about it!

Dear Community Experts,

Did you know? suburban communities are usually located near urban communities or cities. Suburbs are Towns where people. live in homes or apartment buildings. Suburbs have stores to meet the Needs of the residents, but no Large skyscrapers. Some people living in sUburban, communities drive, to other communities or cities to work.

Think about it!

Dear Community Experts,

Did you know Sudbury, located in northern Ontario Is an important forestry And mining community! In 1915 Sudbury provided Most of the worlds nIckel. nickel is used to make many kinds of metal STronger. Sudbury is still one of the world's major, sOurces for nickel. Sudbury is also known for having a major medical centre, Laurentian University? and a science museuM.

Think about it!

Morning Messages: Urban & Rural Communities

Dear Community Experts,

Did you? know that Campbell River is known as "The Salmon Capital of the World". campbell river, british columbia is a town located near Strathcona Provincial Park? People enjoy visiting the area and enjoy the Beautiful Surroundings.

Do you like to eat salmon.!

Think about it!

Dear Community Experts,

Did you know people choose to live In communities for Different Reasons? Some people choose to live in a Place because there is a Job available for them? Some people choose to live in a Place because they like being in a Busy City? Some people choose to live in a Place because they like being close to Nature? Some people live in a place because they have Family and Friends there.?

Think about it!

Dear Community Experts,

Did you know that maps help People find where they need to go! TheRe are All Kinds of maps. Some maps Tell how to get Places? Some Maps tell what The Land formations are. it is very important to Know how to READ a map?

Think about it!

Morning Messages: Urban & Rural Communities

Dear Fishermen,

Did you know peggy's cove is a small Community found in the province of Nova Scotia.? It is located southwest of the City of halifax it is built around a narrow part of The Ocean Shore. Many Jobs in the community have Something to do with the ocean and Fishing.

Happy Fishing!

Dear Foresters,

Did you know the Aboriginal People of fox lake reserve are Cree! This small community is located in Northern ontario. The Population is Under 100 people? The main Industry is forestry other jobs people have on the reserve include secretaries nurses teachers as well as railway and forestry workers The reserve is also Home to a high tech company called Cree-Tech Inc. This company provides Maps and other geographical information to governments and forestry companies across Canada?

Wow!

Dear Community Experts,

Did You Know Baffin Island, Located In The Arctic Region Is Covered In Snow And Ice For Most Of The Year? Even, in the summer, the temperature, is usually, very, cold. Imagine living in Communities Where in the spring you can see whales, walruses and polar bears?!.

Think about it!

Sight Vocabulary Cards

community	urban
rural	town
city	village
hamlet	suburb
goods	services
needs	wants
map	scale

Sight Vocabulary Cards

urban planner	trade
natural resource	physical feature
farm	factory
manufacture	forestry
port	transportation
city worker	reserve
neigbourhood	festival

Urban & Rural Communities

What I think I know........

What I would like to know........

All About Maps

Did you know a **map** is a flat drawing of a place? Maps are used to help people to find the location of a place or thing. Most maps usually have a scale on them. A **scale** is a bar that looks like a ruler. This ruler tells the map reader the real sizes of things and the real distances between places. A **symbol** is a special sign that stands for something that is shown on a map.

There are all kinds of maps. Road maps help people find the best way to travel from place to place. **Road maps** show people major roads, highways and other transportation routes. **Street maps** help people find things within a community like streets, airports, schools, hospitals, stores and parks. Maps can be of a large area like a country or a smaller area like a neighbourhood.

Think about it!

1. Using information from the reading, match and complete each statement.

A. A **symbol** is	or other a small area like a neighbourhood.
B. Road maps show people	a flat drawing of a place.
C. Maps can be of a large area like a country	a special sign that stands for something that is shown on a map.
D. A **scale** is a bar	help people to find the location of a place or thing.
E. Street maps help people find things	major roads, highways and other transportation routes.
F. A **map** is	major roads, highways and other transportation routes.
G. Maps are used to	within a community like streets, airports, schools, hospitals, stores and parks.
H. Road maps show people	that looks like a ruler.

Thinking about: All About Maps

Make a map of your neighbourhood or playground.
Create symbols to help people find things on your map.

Map Symbols

Map of Canada

This is a map of Canada and its provinces and territories.

Think about it!

1. How many provinces are there? _____

2. Name the territories

_____

3. Name the province the furthest east: _____

4. Name the province the furthest west: _____

5. What is the name of your province? _____

Map of Canada

Canada is made up of 10 provinces and 3 territories.
Write the names of the provinces and territories on the map below.
Locate your community and write the name on the map.

Think about it!

I was born in _____ . I live in _____ .

My family chose to live in this community because_____

_____

_____

Mapping Skills

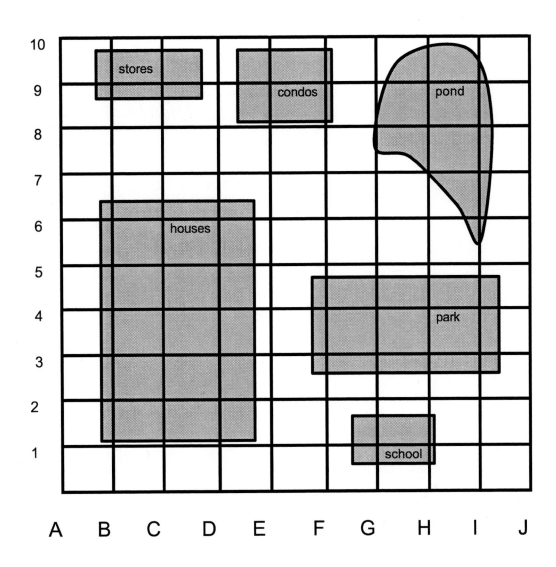

Look at the neighbourhood map. What can be found at these places?

1. (G, 1) _____   2. (C,5) _____

3. (E,9) _____   4. (I,4) _____

6. (H,9) _____   6. (B,3) _____

7. (F,3) _____   8. (D,5) _____

People Need Communities

Did you know that people in communities need or depend on each other? **Needs** are things that people must have to survive. **Wants** are things that people would like, but don't need to survive. Many needs that people have, can be taken care of by themselves. There are also many needs in a community that people would find hard or impossible to do alone, such as build a house or build a car.

1. Fill in the chart below to see how people need communities.
Think about how you get food, mail, electricity, or how the community is kept safe.

Things that people can have or do on their own.	Things it would easier to do or get as a group or community.

2. Using your own ideas, how do you think getting along in a community helps meeting the needs of the community?

_____

_____

_____

Needs and Wants

Think about your community. **Needs** are things that people must have to survive. Needs are things like clean water. **Wants** are things that people would like, but don't need to survive. Wants are things like a sports arena. Sort the list below into needs or wants. Using your own ideas add to the lists. Discuss.

sewage system	movie theatre	city hall	shelter	school
transportation	pet	candy	electricity	roads
restaurant	police	clean water	money	fire department
trips	watch	food	medicine	toys
clean air	friends	television	clothing	playground

Needs	Wants

People Live In Communities

 Did you know Canada has different kinds of communities? A **community** is a place where people live, work and share the same interests. Communities can be small or very large. When people live in a **village**, **reserve** or **hamlet** it is called a **rural community**. When people live in a **town**, **city** or **suburb** it is called an **urban community**.

Rural Communities

Rural communities have lots of open space. There are fewer people and less traffic than there are in towns or cities. People usually live spread out from each other. Sometimes when a few homes are grouped together, it is called a village or hamlet. Some people in rural communities work in jobs related to farming, forestry, mining or fishing.

Urban Communities

Urban communities have lots of people, tall buildings, stores, and lots of cars. People usually live close together or near each other in houses, duplexes or apartment buildings.

Communities are known for different things. Some communities are known for raising crops or livestock, like Lougheed, Alberta. Some communities are known for mining, like Sudbury, Ontario. Some communities are known for lumbering, like Duncan, British Columbia. Some communities are known for fishing, like Bonavista Bay, Newfoundland. Some communities are huge business areas, like Toronto, Ontario. Some communities are located in beautiful areas and are known as tourist destinations like Banff, Alberta.

Thinking about: People Live In Communities

1. Using the information from the reading, write the definitions for the following words.

A. Community

_____

B. Rural Community

_____

C. Urban Community

_____

2. Circle the right answer.

A.	Some people in rural communities work in jobs related to farming, forestry, mining or fishing.	True	False
B.	Urban communities have few people, tall buildings, stores, and lots of cars.	True	False
C.	Communities can be small or very large.	True	False
D.	Rural communities have lots of open space.	True	False
E.	When people live in a village, reserve or hamlet it is called an urban community.	True	False

3. Using the information from the reading, and your own ideas tell what kind of community you live in. Explain your thinking.

_____

_____

Things Found in Urban, Rural or both Kinds of Communities

Cut, sort and paste the pictures below onto the Venn diagram.

road

cow

store

apartment building

people

school

park

subway

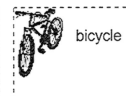
hospital

bicycle

pets

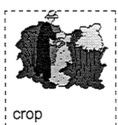
crop

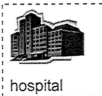
tractor

cityscape

restaurant

flower garden

college

factory

police station

post office

fire truck

grocery store

art gallery

garbage dump

birds

Things Found in Urban, Rural or both Kinds of Communities

Venn-Diagram: This is a diagram of two overlapping circles used to show what two or more sets have in common.

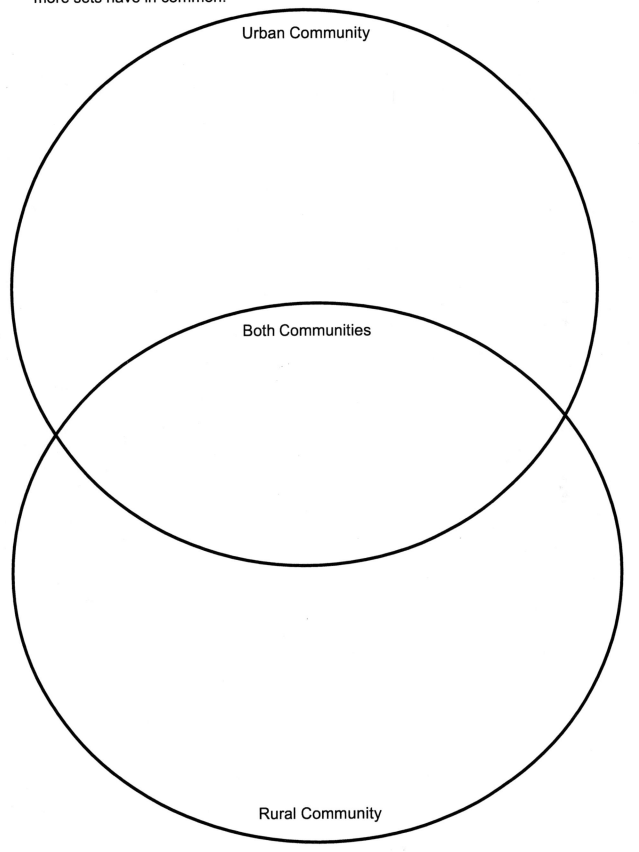

Urban Community

Both Communities

Rural Community

Urban Community Collage

Look through magazines and brochures to find people, places and things found in an urban community. Cut and paste these pictures into a collage in the space below.

Write about your collage.

_____

_____

_____

Rural Community Collage

Look through magazines and brochures to find people, places and things found in a rural community. Cut and paste these pictures into a collage in the space below.

Write about your collage.

_____

_____

_____

Goods and Services

Did you know that goods and services help people to meet their needs and wants? **Goods** are things that people grow, make, or collect, to use or sell. Some examples of goods include vegetables, furniture and lumber. A **service** is a type of helpful work provided to meet the needs of a person or group. A fire fighter and postal worker are examples of people who provide services.

1. Look at the chart below and circle the answer to show if the following things, places or people provide a good or a service.

A. hairdresser	Good	Service	B. library	Good	Service
C. gold	Good	Service	D. police officer	Good	Service
E. shoes	Good	Service	F. spaghetti sauce	Good	Service
G. cereal	Good	Service	H. cookies	Good	Service
I. art gallery	Good	Service	J. teacher	Good	Service
K. cars	Good	Service	L. hospital	Good	Service
M. books	Good	Service	N. public transit	Good	Service
O. gasoline	Good	Service	P. milk	Good	Service
Q. bank	Good	Service	R. ambulance	Good	Service

2. Write the definition for the following.

Goods _____

Service _____

3. Using the information from the reading and your own ideas, how would the goods and services available in an urban community be different from the goods and services in a rural community?

_____

_____

_____

_____

Buying and Selling with Other Communities

Did you know most communities grow, make and sell many different products and services? Many of these products and services are sold to other communities across Canada. When communities trade products and services they become linked. The word **trade** means to give or sell things for something else.

Trade is important because it creates jobs for people in communities. For example, a dairy farmer in a rural community produces milk to sell to a factory in a nearby town. People who work at the factory have jobs such as processing the milk into dairy products like cheese. Next, the factory will sell the dairy products to grocery stores in other communities. Usually trucks are used to transport the dairy products to the grocery stores. People who work in the grocery stores have jobs such as cashiers or managers. The person who buys the cheese from the grocery store is called a consumer. A **consumer** is someone who buys goods or services.

Think about it!

1. Trade means_____.

2. Consumer means _____.

3. Using the information from the reading and your own ideas, explain how trade helps to create jobs.

_____

_____

_____

_____

Activity: Buying and Selling From Other Communities

Fill out the chart:

Name of community we buy from:	What my community buys from there:

What our community sells:	The name of the community that buys from us:

Land and Communities

 Did you know that land plays an important part of how communities develop? Many communities are located where they are today because of available natural resources. **Natural resources** are things that are found in the natural environment and are useful to people. Examples of these things are good soil, water, minerals and forests. Many other communities are where they are today because of their location close to water ways. Waterways made it easier for people to travel and transport goods.

Usually in rural communities a small amount of land is used for homes, stores and other buildings. Most of the land is used for farming, forestry or mining. In urban communities most of the land is used for homes, stores, factories or public places.

As more people move to an urban community, more land is needed to build new homes, roads, and other buildings. This usually means that farmland is bought up. This can become a problem because valuable land is lost to farmers.

Sometimes people like to visit other communities because of a community's physical features. **Physical features** are natural forms found in the environment like mountains, lakes, valleys and rivers. People who like to ski might go to Whistler, British Columbia because of the mountains there. Other people might go to Nova Scotia to live by the ocean.

Think about it!

1. Define natural resources: _____

2. Name 3 examples of natural resources.

_____ _____ _____ _____

Thinking about: Land and Communities

3. Define physical features _____

_____

4. Name 3 examples of physical features.

_____ _____ _____

5. How is land used differently in rural communities than in urban communities? Explain your thinking.

_____

_____

_____

6. What natural resources can be found in or near your community?

_____

_____

_____

_____

7. How do these natural resources affect the way people live in your community?

_____

_____

_____

_____

_____

Farming Communities

 Did you know a farming community usually includes a town and the farms that surround the town? Neighbours in a farming community can live kilometres away from each other. Usually places like, stores, hospitals or places to sell crops, are located in the town.

People in farming communities live in many types of homes. Some people in nearby towns live in apartments above stores, or houses on the street or outside of town. Many families have homes with front and backyards and may have farmland all around. Other people outside of the towns, live on large farms.

There are many types of farms such as dairy, vegetables, cattle, poultry or fruit. Many farms grow a broad range of crops, and still raise animals too. Today most farms use modern technology to help get their work done more easily and quickly. Farm technology like fertilizer, the combine, tractors, temperature controlled sheds and seed drills help farmers do this.

Farmers earn money by selling harvested crops. Farmers get better prices for their crops, such as vegetables, if they are fresh in winter. This is because when fresh vegetables are harder to find, people are willing to pay better prices. Sometimes low rainfall during the growing season creates a smaller crop. This could make the demand for the crop go higher, which can raise prices. Corn is a good example because it is used to make other types of food found in grocery stores.

Farms are very important because they grow and sell crops. These crops may be used to make other food or are sold in markets and grocery stores. Farmers also buy food and goods and services from other communities.

Think about it: Farming Communities

1. Here is a list of different types of farms.

Grows on trees	Grows above ground but not on a tree	Grows Underground	Comes from an animal
Apples	Beans	Beets	Beef
Pears	Corn	Carrots	Cheese
Cherries	Cucumber	Ginger	Chicken
	Lettuce	Onions	Eggs
	Peas	Potatoes	Fish
	Pumpkin	Radishes	Lamb
	Squash	Turnips	Milk
	Strawberries		Pork
	Tomatoes		
	Grapes		
	Watermelon		
	Wheat		

2. If you could have a farm, what kind of farm would you want to have? Explain your choice.

_____

_____

_____

_____

3. Using information from the reading and your own ideas, explain how farms are important to people who live in urban communities.

_____

_____

_____

A Manufacturing Community

 Did you know Oshawa, Ontario has a General Motors auto plant that is bigger than many towns? Oshawa is known as a manufacturing community and makes over a million cars a year. Cars, trucks and other vehicles are an important method of transportation. Vehicles manufactured in Oshawa are sold across Canada and to other countries. Thousands of people from Oshawa work at the plant.

The General Motors auto plant in Oshawa is huge. Not all the people who work there are involved in making vehicles. Some people who work at the plant supply services to other workers. These services include medical, social and food services. Security personnel make sure the plant is a safe place to work. There is even a fire department with a fire truck and fire fighters. Other people work at the offices of General Motors doing marketing, accounting, or other jobs.

Think about it!

What do you think would happen to the community of Oshawa if General Motors moved their plant? Use information from the reading and your own ideas to explain your thinking.

_____

_____

_____

_____

_____

_____

Forestry Communities

Did you know **forestry** is the cutting down and replanting of trees? Trees are a natural resource that is used to make wood products such as paper, boards or furniture. The forest industry provides many jobs for people in communities like Powell River, British Columbia; Meadow Lake, Saskatchewan and White River, Ontario. Products from the forest industry are used by communities across Canada and around the world.

People who live in a community centred on forestry have different types of jobs. Some people work as foresters. Foresters plant, study or harvest trees. Other people work at the sawmill, seed research centre or as part of the fire control unit. Other people have jobs that provide services for the whole community, such as store keepers, policemen, postal workers, restaurateurs, teachers and many more.

Think about it!

1. Define forestry: _____

2. Using information from the reading and your own ideas, explain how forestry affects your daily life.

_____

_____

_____

_____

_____

_____

1. Why is it important to take care of our forests and replant trees?

_____

_____

_____

_____

_____

7. Make a poster of things that come from the forest. You may wish to cut and paste pictures from magazines or draw them.

Port Communities

 Did you know a **port** is a harbour, or place for ships to dock and unload? Well known Canadian port cities include: Montreal, Québec; Vancouver, British Columbia; Halifax, Nova Scotia; Québec City, Québec; St. John's, Newfoundland; and Churchill, Manitoba. Port cities can be found on the east coast, west coast, Hudson Bay and along the St. Lawrence River.

Large ships from Canada and around the world use Canadian ports to transport cargo such as grains, mineral ore and other products. Some of this cargo is then transferred to trains, trucks or airplanes to be delivered across Canada and other parts of North America.

Did you know the St. Lawrence Seaway connects the St. Lawrence River with the Great Lakes? This allows ocean bound vessels to dock at various port cities in the Great Lakes. The St. Lawrence Seaway is only open seasonally. It is closed during the colder months in winter when the St. Lawrence River freezes and ships cannot pass.

Think about it!

1. Define port: _____

2. What happens in port communities?

_____

3. Using information from the reading and your own ideas, why is the St. Lawrence Seaway important?

_____

_____

_____

First Nations Communities

Did you know many First Nations people choose to live in communities called reserves? An **Indian reserve** is land saved for the use of status Indians. **Status Indians** are people who are registered under the Indian Act. Indian reserves are mostly now known as First Nations communities.

First Nations communities are located in both rural and urban areas across Canada. Most reserves are located in rural areas. However, urban reserves can be found in cities like North Vancouver, Capilano or Kahnawake near Montreal. There are very large reserves like the Six Nations Reserve in Ontario or the Peter Ballantyne Reserve in Saskatchewan that have a population of more than 8000 people. As well there are very small reserves that have less than twenty people.

There are six cultural regions of First Nations in Canada. From east to west they are the Woodland First Nations, the Iroquois First Nations, of southeastern Ontario, the Plains First Nations, the Plateau First Nations, the First Nations of the Pacific Coast, and the first Nations of the Mackenzie and Yukon River Basins.

Each First Nations community is special and shows the culture, traditions and language of that nation. Some communities encourage tourism. Some communities are involved in different kinds of industry.

 To learn more about First Nations Communities go to the following website:

http://www.aboriginalcanada.com/firstnation/

Thinking about: First Nations Communities

1. Define the following terms using information from the reading.

A. Indian Reserve: _____

B. Status Indians: _____

2. Name the six cultural regions of First Nations in Canada.

3. Using information from the reading and your own ideas, tell how First Nations Communities are unique.

_____

_____

_____

_____

_____

Brainwork: Go to the website http://www.aboriginalcanada.com/firstnation/

Create a research poster. Make sure you include the following.
- The name of the reserve.
- Where the reserve is located.
- The name of the larger Nation to which the reserve belongs.
- The population.
- The type of industry found in the community.
- Interesting facts.

Mining Communities

Did you know **mining** means the removal of minerals and metals from the Earth? Many things you use in your daily life are made from minerals and metals such as CDs, telephones, computers, trains, cars and medicines.

There lots of different types of jobs in a mining community. Mining engineers design the mine and plan the whole operation. Miners do various jobs to remove the minerals and metals in underground or open pit mines. Miners are also responsible for keeping the workplace safe. There are people who work in the processing and the refinement of the mineral and metals like mineralogists and chemists. Environmental scientists make sure the natural environment is being protected.

A mining operation also needs people who handle the administrative work. These kinds of jobs include receptionists, managers, and other marketing, finance and accounting specialists. There are also people who build and maintain the plant and equipment, such as plumbers, carpenters, welders, truckers, mechanics or electricians.

People who live in a mining community need goods and services. Some people in a mining community work at the grocery stores, restaurants, schools and other places where people can buy goods and services.

Brainwork:

Go to this website and find out where there are mining communities in Canada.

http://mmsd1.mms.nrcan.gc.ca/mmsd/producers/default_e.asp

Metals Mined In Canada

antimony	bismuth	cadmium
calcium	cesium	copper
ilmenite	cobalt	gold
indium	iron ore	lead
lithium	magnesium	zinc
platinum	molybdenum	nickel
tellurium	silver	uranium
selenium	tungsten	tantalum

Non- Metals Mined In Canada

amethyst	asbestos	barite
graphite	bentonite	dolomite
diatomite	diamonds	lime
soapstone	nepheline syenite	mica
potash	talc	pumice
serpentine	gypsum	salt
tremolite	potassium sulphate	sodium sulphate

Check out this website to see where these are mined!

http://mmsd1.mms.nrcan.gc.ca/mmsd/producers/default_e.asp

Research to find out what these non-metals and metals are used for!

Thinking about: Mining Communities

1. Define Mining: _____

2. Using information from the reading and your own ideas, how does mining affect your daily life?

_____

_____

_____

_____

3. Using information from the reading, match and complete each statement.

A. Mining engineers

the removal of minerals and metals from the Earth.

B. Many things you use in your daily life are made from

need goods and services.

C. There are people who work in the processing and the refinement

the natural environment is being protected.

D. Mining means

minerals and metals such as CDs, telephones, computers, trains, cars and medicines.

E. Environmental scientists make sure

design the mine and plan the whole operation.

F. People who live in a mining community

of the mineral and metals like mineralogists and chemists.

4. If you worked in a mining community, what kind job would you choose to do? Why?

_____

_____

_____

Fishing Communities

Did you know Canada has one of the world's most important fishing industries? Canada has the world's longest coastline and is surrounded by the Arctic, Atlantic and Pacific Oceans. Canada is also home to the Great Lakes. Many communities in Canada depend on the fishing industry.

Some fishing communities have large ports, with fish processing plants, transport connections, shipyards and fish research facilities. Other fishing communities are very small and have small anchorages where boats are pulled onto the beach.

The fisheries department decides how much fish can be caught so that there will be enough fish in the years to come and prevents over fishing. **Over fishing** means nature cannot replace all the fish that is caught, quickly enough. The Canadian government also protects the fishing industry by preventing other countries from fishing within 200 nautical miles of Canada's coast.

Aquaculture or fish farming is becoming more popular in rural communities such as in Newfoundland. Fish farmers grow fish in floating sea cages that are anchored to the ocean bottom. Fish farming starts in the hatchery where workers collect fish eggs. Once the eggs hatch, the fish are grown in tanks. Salmon and halibut are two types of fish grown. Farmers sell the fish and seafood they raise to processing plants, grocery stores or restaurants.

Brainwork: Do an Internet search and make a list of the types of fish and seafood found in Canada.

Thinking about: Fishing Communities

1. Why do you think Canada has one the world's most important fishing industries?

_____

_____

_____

2. Define over fishing: _____

3. Do you think the fisheries department has an important job? Explain your thinking using information from the reading and your own ideas.

_____

_____

_____

4. Using information from the reading, match and complete each statement.

A. Fish farmers grow fish in

to processing plants, grocery stores or restaurants.

B. Fish farming starts in

preventing other countries from fishing within 200 nautical miles of Canada's coast.

C. Farmers sell the fish and seafood they raise

floating sea cages that are anchored to the ocean bottom.

D. The Canadian government protects the fishing industry by

with fish processing plants, transport connections, shipyards and fish research facilities.

E. Some fishing communities have large ports,

the hatchery where workers collect fish eggs.

Transportation and Communities

Did you know transportation helps build links between communities? Airplanes, trains, trucks and ships help transport people and deliver goods between communities. Not all communities have the same transportation methods available.

Roads

Canada has many roads. Canada is also home to the longest highway in the world, the Trans-Canada Highway. People sometimes take cars or buses from place to place. Urban communities usually have bus services that run throughout the day. Some smaller communities have bus services that run less often.

Rail

Via Rail is Canada's train system. Many people choose to travel by passenger trains when traveling long distances. Freight trains are also used to transport goods from place to place. Sometimes communities build very fast rail systems to transport people quickly though the city. This is called a subway. Communities with subway systems include: Toronto, Ontario; Montreal Québec; Vancouver, British Columbia and Edmonton, Alberta.

Air

Canada has many airports. People usually choose to travel by air between large distances. In northern communities air travel is very important. Medicines, food and other supplies, as well as people, are transported by air.

Water

The St. Lawrence Seaway is an important source of transportation in Canada. Great quantities of goods like grain and iron ore are moved across long distances by large ships. The St. Lawrence Seaway also allows communities on the Great Lakes to ship goods across the Atlantic Ocean to countries around the world. Some communities have ferries to transport people, like Halifax, Nova Scotia and Victoria, British Columbia.

Thinking about: Transportation and Communities

1. Name three types of transportation.

_____   _____   _____

2. Tell if each statement is true or false.

A.	A subway transports goods across the country.	True	False
B.	In northern communities air travel is very important.	True	False
C.	Transportation helps build links between communities.	True	False
D.	People never use cars or buses if they can fly.	True	False
E.	All communities have the same kind of transportation available.	True	False

3. Using the information from the reading and your own ideas, tell how transportation is important. Explain your thinking.

_____

_____

_____

_____

4. What kind of transportation links does your community have?

_____

_____

_____

_____

Transportation Survey

What kind of transportation links do you use? Conduct a survey of your classmates.

Type of Transportation																				
Walk																				
Bicycle																				
School bus																				
Public Bus																				
Subway																				
Train																				
Car																				
Airplane																				

Number of Students

What is the most popular method of transportation? _____

How does your community's natural environment affect transportation used by people?

_____

_____

_____

_____

Cities

Did you know a city is a large urban community? Many people choose to live in a city for different reasons. Some people live in a city because they enjoy the available services. Some people live in a city because it is close to their work. Some people live in a city because that is where they were born.

Each city is unique. Often cities were built near natural resources or important transportation routes like rivers. Usually cities have industry, manufacturing, stores, government buildings, hospitals, museums, shopping malls, sports arenas, and schools.

Cities can be many sizes. Some cities have thousands of people like Moncton, New Brunswick or Red Deer, Alberta. Some cities even have more than a million people like Toronto, Ontario or Montreal, Québec. People in cities may live in houses, apartment buildings, townhouses, duplexes or other buildings.

Depending on the city, people have different choices for transportation. Some people drive their own cars. Some people use the public transit system which may include a subway. Some people may ride their bikes or walk to where they need to go.

City workers do jobs that help keep the city running. Some of these city workers include police officers, postal workers, firefighters, sanitation workers and government officials. There are also people who work to make sure there is enough clean water and electricity for the whole community to use.

Sometimes air pollution, water waste, electricity shortages and too much garbage can be a problem in a city. People are encouraged to conserve energy by not driving as much, using less water and turning off lights! Many cities also have recycling programs to reduce the amount of garbage.

Thinking about: Cities

1. List three reasons why people may choose to live in a city.

_____

_____

_____

2. Tell if each statement is true or false.

A.	Often cities were built near natural resources or important transportation routes like rivers.	True	False
B.	Few cities have recycling programs to reduce the amount of garbage.	True	False
C.	City workers do jobs that help keep the city running.	True	False
D.	Depending on the city, people have different choices for transportation.	True	False
E.	People in cities live only in apartment buildings.	True	False
F.	Cities come in many sizes.	True	False

3. Using information from the reading and your ideas, why do you think city workers are important to a city?

_____

_____

_____

_____

4. Would you like to live in a city? Explain your opinion.

_____

_____

_____

Canada Capital City Word Search

F	R	E	D	E	R	I	C	T	O	N	J	H
W	H	I	T	E	H	O	R	S	E	G	H	A
R	S	R	T	H	W	T	E	R	S	F	I	L
E	D	M	O	N	T	O	N	V	Y	J	Q	I
G	Q	A	Z	X	C	R	G	I	U	V	A	F
I	W	A	F	T	D	O	U	C	N	M	L	A
N	K	L	O	P	R	N	R	T	O	T	U	X
A	X	F	G	H	J	T	Y	O	I	Q	I	M
T	S	E	Q	T	U	O	H	R	B	M	T	K
Y	E	L	L	O	W	K	N	I	F	E	U	I
S	T	J	O	H	N	S	M	A	D	L	L	O
Q	W	E	O	T	T	A	W	A	J	M	N	P
W	I	N	N	I	P	E	G	B	I	N	B	H
Q	U	É	B	E	C	C	I	T	Y	Y	V	G
C	H	A	R	L	O	T	T	E	T	O	W	N

OTTAWA	IQALUIT	VICTORIA	YELLOWKNIFE
ST.JOHNS	HALIFAX	WHITEHORSE	TORONTO
EDMONTON	QUÉBEC CITY	REGINA	WINNIPEG

Match the capital city to its country, province or territory.

Canada	Victoria
Nunavut	Québec City
Yukon	Ottawa
British Columbia	Toronto
Alberta	Edmonton
Saskatchewan	Yellowknife
Manitoba	St. John's
Ontario	Halifax
Québec	Regina
Prince Edward Island	Iqaluit
New Brunswick	Winnipeg
Nova Scotia	Whitehorse
Newfoundland and Labrador	Victoria

All About Urban Planning

Did you know **urban planners** have the job of planning how and where a community grows? Urban planners help imagine the effects on a community as it grows. Urban planners work in cooperation with communities to plan where areas for neighborhoods, factories, stores, schools, parks and other buildings should be built.

The goal of urban planning is to maintain well organized growth in urban communities and to correct any fast uncontrolled growth. Urban planners recommend the best places to build things like a sports arena, parking lot or a new factory. Urban planners also keep track of where things are built to make sure that there are enough sewer systems, roads, stores, parks and green spaces for people living in a community.

A well planned community usually has a nice shopping area, lots of parks and open spaces so people don't feel crowded.

Poorly planned communities often have factories, houses and shopping areas mixed together. This often makes a community feel crowded.

Think about it!

1. Using information from the reading, match and complete each statement.

A. Poorly planned communities often	maintain well organized growth in urban communities and to correct any fast uncontrolled growth.
B. Urban planners help imagine	to plan how and where a community grows.
C. A well planned community usually has	to build things like a sports arena and parking lot or a new factory.
D. The goal of urban planning is to	have factories, houses and shopping areas mixed together.
E. Urban planners have the job	nice shopping area lots of parks, and open spaces so people don't feel crowded.
F. Urban planners recommend the best places	the effects on a community as it grows.

Thinking about: All About Urban Planning

2. List all things you most like and dislike about your community. Think about things like parks, factories, shopping areas, green spaces, school etc.

Things I like about my community.	Things I don't like about my community.

3. Using the information from the reading and your own ideas, tell how you would change your community. Explain your thinking.

_____

_____

_____

_____

_____

_____

_____

_____

_____

Canadian Community Celebrations and Festivals

Did you know that many communities across Canada are known for their special celebrations and festivals? Each community is unique. Some celebrations are based on the community's heritage. Some celebrations are based on the type of food grown there. Community celebrations and festivals encourage people to be proud of where they live. Here are some examples:

Place?	Name of Celebration or Festival?	What happens?
Brighton, Ontario	Applefest http://www.applefest.reach.net/	Baking contests, arts and crafts.
Québec City, Québec	Carnaval De Québec http://www.carnaval.qc.ca/	Winter carnival, ice sculptures, contests.
Calgary, Alberta	Calgary Exhibition and Stampede http://calgarystampede.com/	Wild West rodeo and stampede.
Shediac, New Brunswick	Shediac Lobster Festival http://www.lobsterfestival.nb.ca/	Celebrating "the lobster capital of the world".
St. John's, Newfoundland	Newfoundland and Labrador Folk Festival http://www.sjfac.nf.net/	A cultural showcase.
Dawson City, Yukon	Dawson City Discovery Days http://www.dawsoncity.org/index.php	Celebration of the Klondike gold discovery.
Regina, Saskatchewan	Western Canada International Pow Wow	Celebration of native crafts, and foods.
Vancouver, British Columbia	Alcan Dragon Boat Festival http://www.adbf.com/	Chinese dragon boat races.
Kentville, Nova Scotia	Annapolis Valley Apple Blossom Festival http://www.appleblossom.com/	Parades, dances and sports and food activities.
Bala, Ontario	Bala Cranberry Festival http://www.balacranberryfestival.on.ca/	Marsh tours, midway rides, and arts and crafts.

Many people from other communities come to these celebrations or festivals to join in the fun. Check out some of these websites and write a journal about where you would like to go and why.

Thinking about: Canadian Community Celebrations and Festivals

1. Make a list of special events, celebrations, or festivals that happen in your community and tell why each one is special.

Event, celebration or festival	Why does it happen?

2. Which event, celebration or festival is your favourite? Explain your opinion.

_____

_____

_____

 Brainwork: Bring in pictures, postcards or other artifacts of your favourite celebration to share with your class.

Comparison Community Map

Name of Community

Name of Community

Information

Information

Comparing…

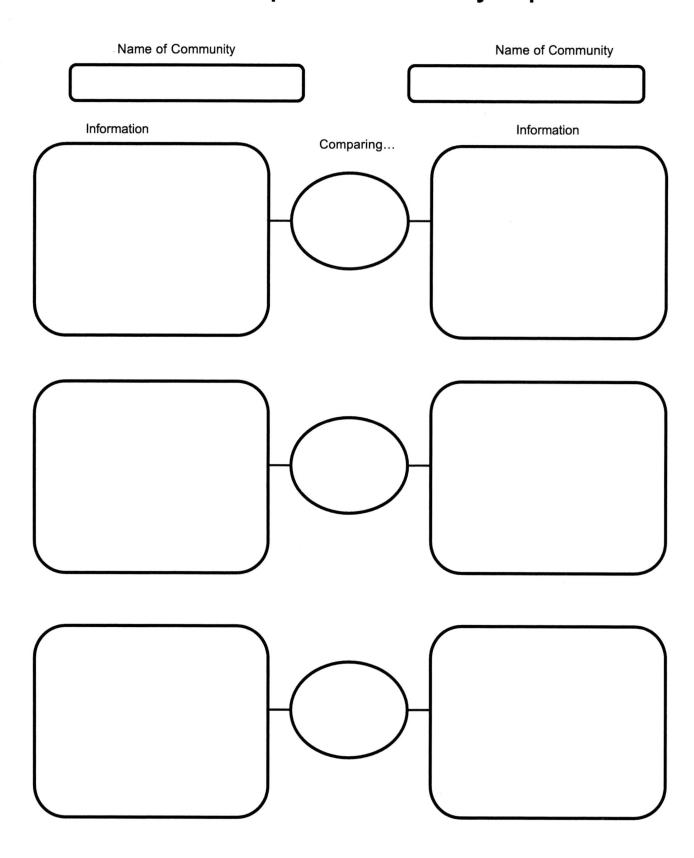

Community Research

Name of community _____

Type of Community Urban or Rural? What is the community known for? What is the population?	
Transportation What types of transportation are found in this community?	
Products / Industry What kind of jobs do most people have in this community?	
Recreation What do people like to do in this community?	
Tourist Attractions What kinds of places do people like to visit?	
Interesting Facts	

Comparing Communities

Compare......		
Location		
Population		
Transportation		
Housing		
Industry		
Services		

Community Postcard

Pretend you went to visit another community. Write a postcard to a friend.

Community Scavenger Hunt

Name a rural community.	Name the capital of your province.	Name a community known for fishing.	Name a reserve community.
Name a manufacturing community.	Name a community with a subway system.	Name an urban community.	Name a community you would like to visit.
Name a community known for forestry.	Name a community that is similar to yours.	Name a community near mountains.	Name the capital of Canada.
Name a community near water.	Name a community with a very cold climate.	Name a farming community.	Name a community that is different from yours.

Culminating Activity: Urban & Rural Communities

The purpose of these culminating activities is to create a real world connection for students when learning about urban and rural communities. This encourages application of concepts learned. These activities may be done as:

- a whole group
- small group
- individual project
- home project

Use the cards and black line masters as suggested activities. The teacher may choose to make accommodations for individual students by choosing or omitting appropriate cards to match the student's level.

Teacher Tips:

- Brainstorm a class list of qualities that make a good project, for example large neat printing, clear labels, colourful pictures.

- Model for the students how to complete each of the activity cards. Provide examples of quality work.

- Share completed projects with other classes, parents and other members of the community.

Culminating Activity Cards

Urban Planning: Community Map

You and your friends have been chosen by the **Future Urban Planners of Canada** to design the ultimate urban community. Your community is by a fresh-water unpolluted lake. Create a map of your community. A **map** is a flat drawing of a place. Maps are used to help people to find the location of a place or thing. A **symbol** is a special sign that stands for something that is shown on a map.

What you need:

- Large piece of construction paper or poster board.
- Symbols of the community buildings and areas.
- Colouring pencils and markers.
- Scissors, and glue.

What you do:

1. Cut out the symbols to be pasted onto your community map.
2. Plan your community. Think about where to place buildings and areas on your map.
3. Make sure:
   - ✓ Your map is labeled neatly.
   - ✓ You use a ruler for your roads.
   - ✓ You print neatly.
   - ✓ Your map has the compass points.

Urban Planning: Community Symbols

 airport

 factory

 store

 apartment building

 apartment building

 park

 park

 subway

 pet clinic

 hotel

 city hall

 office buildings

 play ground

 public library

 entertainment arena

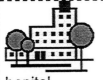 hopital

 college

 space observatory

 police station

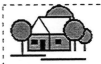 post office

 homes

 homes

 homes

 homes

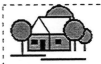 homes

 restaurant

 restaurant

 store

 store

grocery store

Urban Planning: Community Symbols

Extra Tips

When placing the community symbols on your map, think about:

- Do I want to add any ponds or rivers to my community?

- Does my community need any bridges?

- Where will I put the roads and how will they be shaped?

- What kinds of buildings and areas do I want near each other? Talk about it with a friend.

- Where would be a good place for the garbage dump?

- Where should public places like the train station and entertainment centre go?

Culminating Activity Cards

Urban and Rural Communities Activity Card

Make a Poster

There are many different types of posters. Here are some examples:

- **Research Posters**: tell facts about something.
- **Advertising Posters**: try to sell you something, like a product made in your community.
- **Information Posters**: tell you a message, like "keep our community clean!"
- **Travel Posters**: tell you about a place you might like to visit.

Choose a type of poster from the list and make a poster related to your community.

Urban and Rural Communities Activity Card

Pretend that you can spend a day in another community such as one of the provincial capital cities. Choose three communities you would want to visit. Write about the following:

- Why would you want to go there?
- What would you do?
- What are some interesting facts about that city?

Here is a link to provincial websites that will help you find a community to visit.
http://canada.gc.ca/othergov/prov_e.html

Here is a link to provincial capital cities websites.
http://www.capitaleducanada.gc.ca/ccco/index_e.asp

Culminating Activity Cards

Urban and Rural Communities Activity Card
Create A Community Model

Choose to make a model urban or rural community. Brainstorm a list of buildings and areas found in the type of community you have chosen to do:

What you need:
- old boxes, milk cartons, paper tubes
- construction paper
- scissors
- tape and glue
- paint mixed with liquid detergent so that it sticks to the boxes or milk cartons
- crayons and markers
- green tissue paper

Optional: toy vehicles, and miniature people, pieces of pine tree for forests etc.

What you do:
1. Use the found materials to create buildings for your community.
2. Use tissue paper for trees, rivers or lakes.
3. Use your imagination!
4. Write about your community, explaining the different parts.

Urban and Rural Communities Activity Card
Community Brochure

Create a brochure about the community of your choice. A brochure is a pamphlet that gives information. In your brochure include things like:

- Places to visit.
- Location and population.
- Interesting facts.
- For what your community is known.
- A list of types of services found in your community.

What's Your Opinion?

Use the following questions as journal prompts for students. You may also wish to use these questions as discussion starters.

1. Would you rather live in a rural community or an urban community? Tell why.

2. Would you rather live in a place that has lots of outdoor activities available like mountains for skiing or lakes for swimming or live in a place that has lots of indoor activities available like movie theatres, art classes and special shows. Tell Why.

3. Would you rather live in a quiet place or a noisy place? Tell why?

4. Do you think it is o.k. to let cities grow bigger and lose farmland?

5. Describe ways you and your family use the natural environment. For example, gardening, or going to the park.

6. Do you think it is important to reduce, reuse and recycle in a community? Explain your thinking.

7. What can you do to keep your community clean?

8. What would make your community a better place to live?

9. Do you think when communities exchange goods with other communities they become a better place to live?

10. Do you think farming communities should grow larger?

11. How are community workers important to making your community a nice place to live?

Community Class Scrapbook

Dear Parents and Guardians,

Over the course of our study of Urban and Rural Communities, please help your child collect maps, newspaper articles, magazine articles, flyers, government pamphlets, tourist brochures, Internet site lists etc., that have to do with our community.

The purpose of this project is to help children gain a better understanding of how our community is unique. Descriptions, lists and artifacts will be added to our class community scrapbook.

Here are additional ideas of things to collect or write about.

A map of your community.	A picture of a famous person from your community.	The name of your representative in government.	The name of the next closest community.	Something from a place where you go to have fun.
A retell of how your family chose to settle in this community.	A list of businesses found in your community.	Describe an historical event from your community.	The name of the street you live on.	Names of animals found in your community.
The name of the closest airport to your community.	Describe a festival or special event that happens in your community.	A list of community helpers found in your community.	Something that shows the best thing about your community.	The name of the closest body of water to your community.
A list of types of transportation found in your community along with ticket stubs.	A list of community events.	Something to show what product or service your community is known for.	Something to show for what your community is famous.	A picture of your home.
How does your community change from the winter to summer?	Something that shows the place where your town's water comes from.	Something that shows the worst thing about your community.	A rubbing of a tree leaf or plant found in your community.	A weather and climate report for your community.

Your participation in our community scrapbook is greatly appreciated!

Urban and Rural Communities Activity Card

Sound Scape

A sound scape imitates sounds found in life. Pretend you are in a busy urban community. Brainstorm a list of sounds you might hear. Pretend you are in a rural community. Brainstorm a list of sounds you might hear. How are the noises the same or different?

1. Find at least four friends and choose a community environment to imitate.
2. Assign different sounds from that community to each person in your group.
3. Practise making the sound.
4. When the leader of your group or teacher gives the signal make the sound.

Acrostic Poem

1. Write the name of your community down the side of the page.
2. Think of a word or phrase to describe your community and write it after each letter.
3. Start each word or phrase using each letter of the name of your community as the beginning.

For example: **T**errific place to live.

Open for many businesses

We have lots to do and see here

Never going to leave!

Be a Community Reporter

Usually communities have a local newspaper. Pretend you are a newspaper reporter and a write an article about your community. Here are some suggestions:

- a sports story
- a community event
- an interview with a community leader
- a historical event

These are the parts of a news story you need to know:
- The **HEADLINE** names the story.
- The **BYLINE** shows the name of the author. (You)
- The **BEGINNING** gives the most important idea.
- The **MIDDLE** tells more about the story.
- The **ENDING** gives the reader and idea to remember.

Newspaper Article Checklist:

Grammar and Style

☐ I used my neatest writing and included a clear title.

☐ I included a colourful picture.

☐ I checked for spelling.

☐ I used interesting words.

☐ I checked for capitals, periods, commas and question marks.

Content

☐ I have a **HEADLINE** that names the story.

☐ I have a **BYLINE** that shows my name as the author.

☐ I have a **BEGINNING** that gives the most important facts.

☐ I have a **MIDDLE** part that tells details about the story.

☐ I have an **ENDING** that gives the reader an idea to remember.

Art Activity: Cityscape

In this art activity, create a cityscape. Children can explore lines in their environment.

What you need:
- Black construction paper
- Newspaper
- Glue
- Ruler
- Scissors
- Pencil

What you do:
1. Discuss with children the idea that from far away a group of buildings looks like vertical blocks. Use pictures of cityscapes to support the concept if possible;
2. Reinforce the concept of a horizon line with demonstrations on the blackboard;
3. Show children how to use the ruler to create a horizon line on the black construction paper;
4. Show children how to cut out along the printed columns of the newspaper (these will become the buildings for the cityscape);
5. Distribute the materials to the children and allow them to construct their cityscape.

Discussion question:

Discuss with children how their homes compare to their cityscape. What do they see when they look out their window?

Urban and Rural Communities Word Search

```
R U K C C U U W T G A E Y R E
R E T A W G O R C Z C G R O V
Y R T S E R O F B I V A O A R
E N R Y R Y G Y F A M L T D E
R I E U T O W I O A N L C P S
A A R E O I S Y N Y N I A A E
G A I D D H C U T E M V F N R
L S S L E S F I V P C T O W N
C T X R V A N S E R V I C E S
A N Y Z C U V R Z E B V J E M
D A H T M G X I A N R M E R T
S W U M N I Z S P I U C A R V
C R O T E L M A H M B F O Z O
E C Y M Z K U U U C U P R H P
T W U I K P T J S P S F S N W
```

AIR	CITY	COMMUNITY	FACTORY
FISHERY	FORESTRY	HAMLET	MANUFACTURE
PORT	RAIL	RESERVE	ROAD
SUBURB	TOWN	URBAN	VILLAGE
GOODS	SERVICES	NEEDS	WANTS
FARM	MINE	RURAL	WATER

Urban and Rural Communities: Unit Test

Carefully read each question. Fill in the bubble with the **best** answer for each question.

1. A **community** is _____.
   - ○ a place where people live, work and share the same interests.
   - ○ a place where people eat and drink.
   - ○ a type of place.
   - ○ none of the above.

2. A **map** is _____.
   - ○ a picture.
   - ○ a flat drawing of a place.
   - ○ a type of paper.
   - ○ none of the above.

3. A **need** is _____.
   - ○ something that a person does not need to survive.
   - ○ something that a person needs to survive.
   - ○ something that a community does not provide.
   - ○ none of the above.

4. When people live in a **town**, **city** or **suburb** it is called _____.
   - ○ a country.
   - ○ a rural community.
   - ○ an urban community.
   - ○ none of the above.

5. **Goods** are things that
   - ○ people don't need to survive.
   - ○ people talk about.
   - ○ people grow, make, or collect to use or sell.
   - ○ none of the above.

Urban and Rural Communities: Unit Test

Carefully read each question. Fill in the bubble with the **best** answer for each question.

6. When people live in a **village**, **reserve** or **hamlet** it is called a _____.

○ a rural community.

○ an urban community.

○ a country.

○ none of the above.

7. **Wants** are things that._____.

○ people can not have.

○ people need to survive.

○ people would like, but don't need to survive.

○ none of the above.

8. **Urban planners** have the job to _____.

○ plan how and where a community grows.

○ plan festivals and celebrations.

○ buy land in rural communities.

○ none of the above.

9. List 6 different types of communities.

Urban and Rural Communities: Unit Test

10. Using the information you have learned, and your own ideas fill in the chart.

Compare......	Rural community	Urban community
Population		
Transportation		
Housing		
Industry		
Services		

Urban and Rural Communities: Unit Test

11. Using information you have learned and your own ideas, explain how communities need each other.

Self- Evaluation: What I Learned

The best part of the unit was……

_____

_____

_____

I learned about……..

_____

_____

_____

I want to learn more about….

_____

_____

_____

My Work Habits:

	Yes	Sometimes	I need to try harder.
I listened to the teacher.			
I tried my best to work on my own.			
I did neat work with lots of details.			
I was a good group member.			
I did my work on time and with care.			

Rubric: Student Self-Assessment

A	WOW	✓ I completed my work independently on time and with care. ✓ I added details and followed the instructions without help. ✓ I understand and can talk about what I have learned.
B	BRAVO	✓ I completed my work on time and with care. ✓ I followed the instructions with almost no help. ✓ I understand and can talk about what I have learned.
C	OKAY	✓ I completed my work. ✓ I followed the instructions with some help. ✓ I understand and can talk about most of what I have learned.
D	UH-OH	✓ I need to complete my work on time and with care. ✓ I should ask for help when I need it. ✓ I understand and can talk about a few of the things that I have learned.

Post the above rubric in your classroom to assist children in self- evaluation and direction for improvement in completing the tasks assigned.

Student Assessment Rubric

	Level One	Level Two	Level Three	Level Four
BASIC CONCEPTS	• Shows little of understanding of concepts. • Rarely gives complete explanations. • Teacher support is intensive.	• Shows some understanding of concepts. • Gives appropriate, but incomplete explanations. • Some teacher assistance is needed.	• Shows understanding of most concepts. • Usually gives complete or nearly complete explanations. • Infrequent teacher support is needed.	• Shows understanding of all or almost all concepts. • Consistently gives appropriate and complete explanations independently. • No teacher support is needed.
COMMUNICATION	• Rarely communicates with clarity and precision in written and oral work. • Rarely uses appropriate terminology and vocabulary. • Intensive teacher prompts needed to use correct vocabulary.	• Sometimes communicates with clarity and precision in written and oral work. • Rarely uses appropriate terminology and vocabulary. • Occasional teacher prompts needed to use correct vocabulary.	• Usually communicates with clarity and precision in written and oral work. • Usually uses appropriate terminology and vocabulary. • Infrequent teacher prompts needed to use correct vocabulary.	• Consistently communicates with clarity and precision in written and oral work with supporting details. • Consistently uses appropriate terminology and vocabulary. • No teacher prompts needed to use correct vocabulary.
CONCEPT APPLICATION	• Student displays little understanding or comparing urban and rural communities. • Rarely applies concepts and skills in a variety of contexts. • Intensive teacher support is needed to encourage application of concepts.	• Student sometimes displays understanding or comparing urban and rural communities. • Sometimes applies concepts and skills in a variety of contexts. • Occasional teacher support is needed to encourage application of concepts.	• Student usually displays understanding of connecting or comparing urban and rural communities. • Usually applies concepts and skills in a variety of contexts. • Infrequent teacher support is needed to encourage application of concepts.	• Student consistently displays understanding of connecting or comparing urban and rural communities. • Almost always applies concepts and skills in a variety of contexts. • No teacher support is needed to encourage application of concepts.

Student Evaluation Sheet

Activity Completed	Grade

General Comments:

_____

_____

_____

Urban & Rural Communities: Fantastic Websites

http://atlas.gc.ca/site/english/learningresources/ccatlas/index.html

The Canadian Communities Atlas offers a unique national network of geographic information by providing schools the opportunity to create an internet-based atlas of their community.

http://www.ext.vt.edu/resources/4h/virtualfarm/main.html

This is an excellent website for students to explore different kinds of farming. By exploring this website students will gain a better understanding of how farming affects their daily lives.

http://www.whitebirch.ca/kids/kids.shtml

This is a great website sponsored by the Saskatchewan Forestry Association. This site provides interesting information about forestry and with a special section for kids.

http://www.epa.gov/recyclecity/

This is a great interactive website for students to learn about recycling at Recycle City.

http://www.aboriginalcanada.com/firstnation/

This is an informative website that allows you to navigate through a directory of several First Nations community websites.

http://www.lizardpoint.com/fun/geoquiz/canquiz.html

This is fun website where students can test their knowledge of where provinces and territories are located on a map.

http://ceps.statcan.ca/english/profil/placesearchform1.cfm

This government website allows students to find out information about any community in Canada. A mapping feature is also available.

http://www.econedlink.org/lessons/index.cfm?lesson=EM194

This website is sponsored by the National Council on Economic Education in the United States. This webpage allows the kids to take part in interactive lessons on the types of goods of services that businesses offer.

http://pbskids.org/rogers/

The Mister Rogers Neighorhood website has sections where kids can build their own neighbourhood or take a factory tour to see how things are made.

http://www.nrcan.gc.ca/mms/wealth/intro-e.htm

This government website allows students to take a tour of spaces in the home and identifies minerals used in many household items.

Urban & Rural Communities Expert

Keep up the quality work!

Quality Community Planner

Great Work!